THIS BLOOMSBURY BOOK

BELONGS TO

....

For Eleanor, Lizzie, and Andrew

First published in Great Britain in 2005 by Bloomsbury Publishing Plc
This paperback edition first published in 2006
50 Bedford Square, London, WC1B 3DP
Text copyright © Dosh Archer 2005
Illustrations copyright © Dosh Archer and Mike Archer 2005
The moral rights of Dosh Archer and Mike Archer to be identified
as the author and illustrators have been asserted

ISBN 9780747579298

Printed in China by South China Printing Company, Dongguan City, Guangdong

10 9 8 7 6 5 4 3

Looking
After
Little
Ellie

written and illustrated by
Dosh and Mike Archer

BLOOMSBURY

LONDON BERLIN NEW YORK SYDNEY

When Flora rang to ask us to come
and look after Little Ellie,
we said yes.
You have to help your friends.

It was the first time we had
looked after Little Ellie.

Flora said she would be back soon.

But when her mum left,
Little Ellie got a bit upset.

So we did our best to cheer her up.

We gave her
some lunch,

changed her nappy,

and took her to the park.

We played on the swing,

and the see-saw.

We sang for her and danced for her,

and then she had a nap.
She looked really sweet
when she was asleep.

Then it was time to go home.

When she got back, Flora said,
'I hope she hasn't been any trouble.'

'Not a bit,' we said,
as we kissed Ellie goodbye.

It's been a big day, but we don't mind.
After all, she's just a little baby.

Also by
Dosh and Mike Archer ...